For Sally and Bob

Dear Parents:

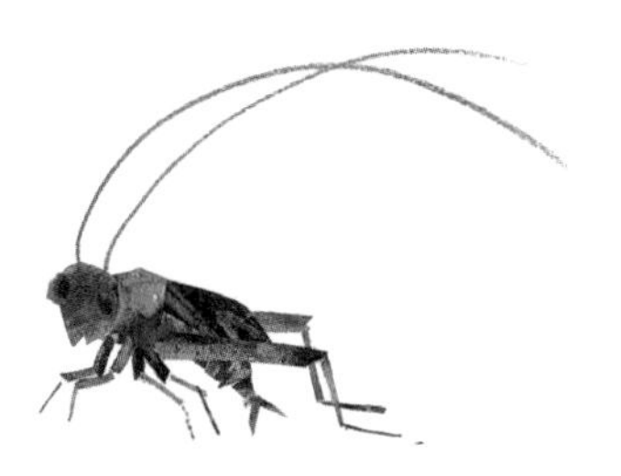

Congratulations! Your child is taking the first steps on an exciting journey. The destination? Independent reading!

STEP INTO READING® will help your child get there. The program offers five steps to reading success. Each step includes fun stories and colorful art or photographs. In addition to original fiction and books with favorite characters, there are Step into Reading Non-Fiction Readers, Phonics Readers and Boxed Sets, Sticker Readers, and Comic Readers—a complete literacy program with something to interest every child.

Learning to Read, Step by Step!

Ready to Read Preschool–Kindergarten
• big type and easy words • rhyme and rhythm • picture clues
For children who know the alphabet and are eager to begin reading.

Reading with Help Preschool–Grade 1
• basic vocabulary • short sentences • simple stories
For children who recognize familiar words and sound out new words with help.

Reading on Your Own Grades 1–3
• engaging characters • easy-to-follow plots • popular topics
For children who are ready to read on their own.

Reading Paragraphs Grades 2–3
• challenging vocabulary • short paragraphs • exciting stories
For newly independent readers who read simple sentences with confidence.

Ready for Chapters Grades 2–4
• chapters • longer paragraphs • full-color art
For children who want to take the plunge into chapter books but still like colorful pictures.

STEP INTO READING® is designed to give every child a successful reading experience. The grade levels are only guides; children will progress through the steps at their own speed, developing confidence in their reading. The F&P Text Level on the back cover serves as another tool to help you choose the right book for your child.

Remember, a lifetime love of reading starts with a single step!

Visit us on the Web!
StepIntoReading.com
rhcbooks.com

Educators and librarians, for a variety of teaching tools, visit us at
RHTeachersLibrarians.com

Library of Congress Cataloging-in-Publication Data is available upon request.
ISBN 978-0-593-43232-7 (trade) — ISBN 978-0-593-43233-4 (lib. bdg.)

Printed in the United States of America
10 9 8 7 6 5 4 3 2 1

This book has been officially leveled by using the F&P Text Level Gradient™ Leveling System.

STEP 3 READING ON YOUR OWN

STEP INTO READING®

world of ERIC CARLE™

The Very Quiet Cricket

by Eric Carle

Random House New York

One warm day, from a tiny egg

a little cricket was born.

Welcome! chirped a big cricket,

rubbing his wings together.

The little cricket wanted to answer,

so he rubbed his wings together.

But nothing happened.

Not a sound.

Good morning! whizzed a locust,

spinning through the air.

The little cricket wanted

to answer, so he rubbed

his wings together.

But nothing happened.

Not a sound.

Hello! whispered a praying mantis, scraping its huge front legs together.

The little cricket wanted

to answer, so he rubbed

his wings together.

But nothing happened.

Not a sound.

Good day! crunched a worm,

munching its way out of

an apple.

The little cricket wanted to

answer, so he rubbed

his wings together.

But nothing happened.

Not a sound.

Hi! bubbled a spittlebug,

slurping in a sea of froth.

The little cricket wanted to

answer, so he rubbed

his wings together.

But nothing happened.

Not a sound.

Good afternoon!
screeched a cicada,
clinging to a branch
of a tree.
The little cricket
wanted to answer,
so he rubbed his
wings together.

But nothing happened.

Not a sound.

How are you! hummed
a bumblebee, flying from
flower to flower.
The little cricket wanted
to answer, so he rubbed his
wings together.
But nothing happened.
Not a sound.

Good evening! whirred a dragonfly, gliding above the water.

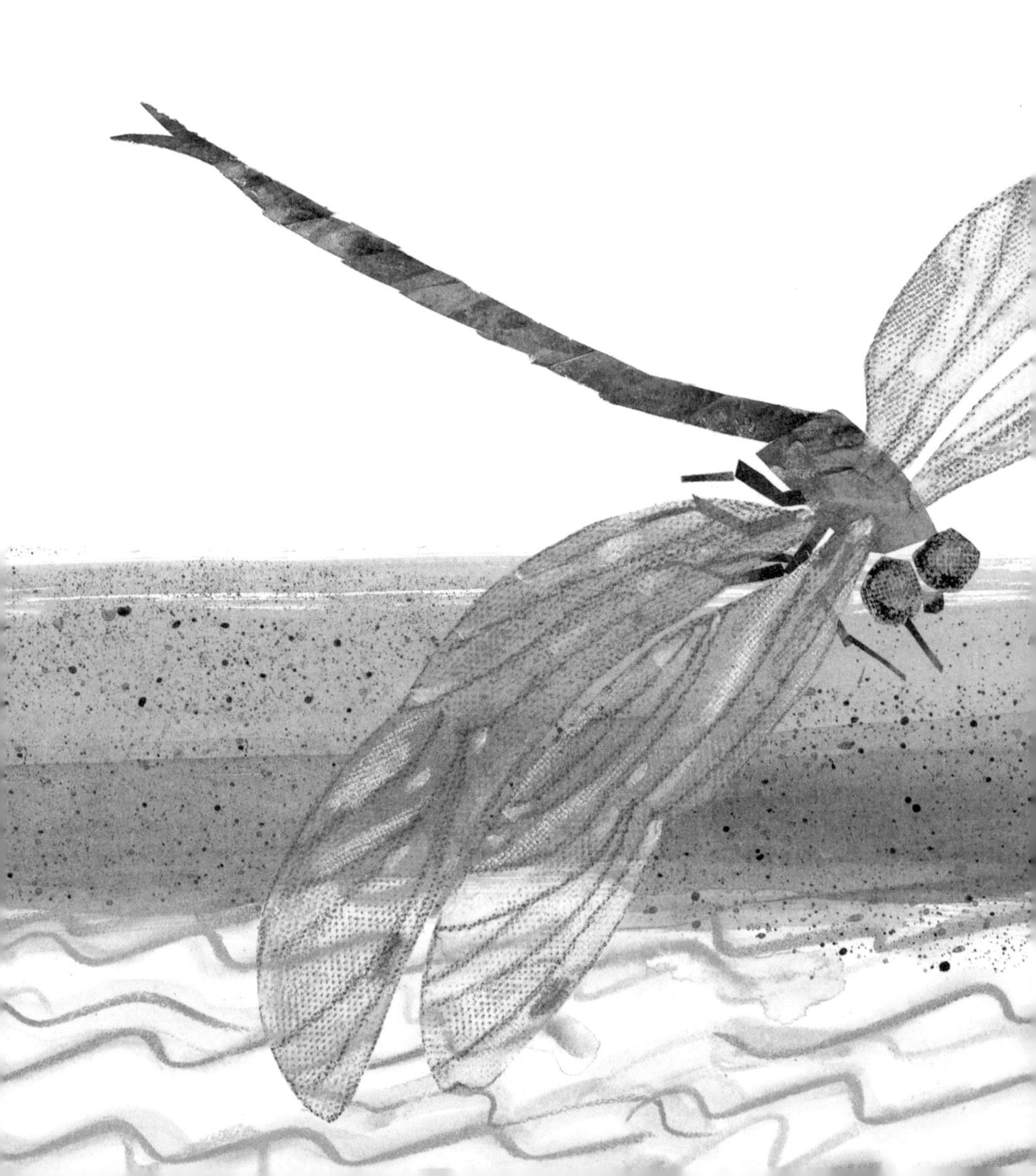

The little cricket wanted to answer,

so he rubbed his wings together.

But nothing happened.

Not a sound.

Good night! buzzed the mosquitoes, dancing among the stars.

The little cricket wanted to answer,

so he rubbed his wings together.

But nothing happened.

Not a sound.

A luna moth sailed quietly
through the night.

And the cricket enjoyed
the stillness.

As the luna moth disappeared
silently into the distance,
the cricket saw another cricket.

She, too, was a very quiet cricket.

Then he rubbed his wings

together one more time.

And this time he chirped the most beautiful sound that she had ever heard.

There are 4,000 different
kinds of crickets.
Some live underground,
others above.
Some live in shrubs or trees,
and some even live in water.

Both male and female crickets can hear, but only the male can make a sound.

By rubbing his wings together he chirps. Some people say that it sounds like a song!

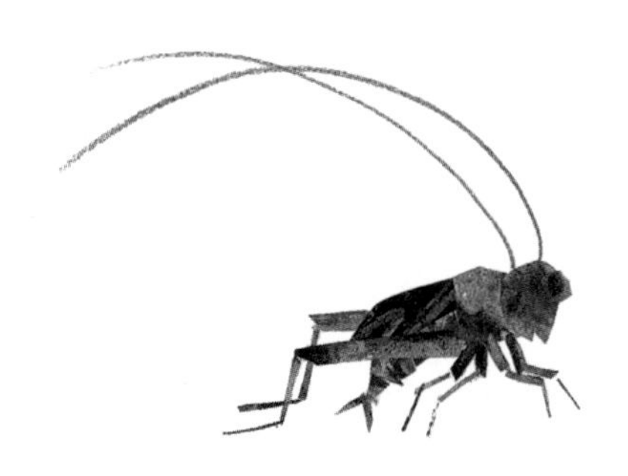